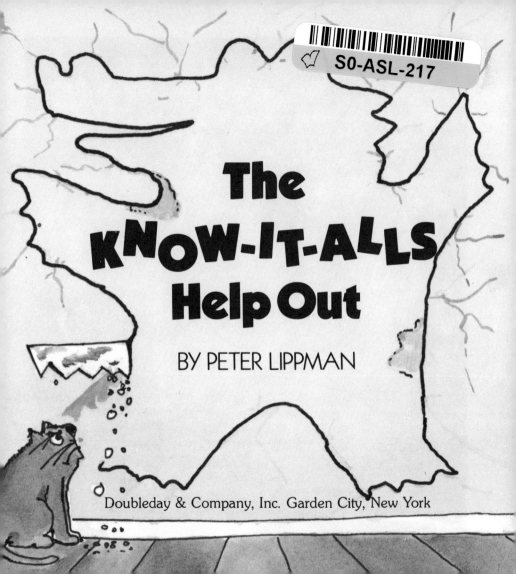

The KNOW-IT-ALLS Help Out

BY PETER LIPPMAN

Doubleday & Company, Inc. Garden City, New York

Library of Congress Catalog Card Number 81-43431
Library of Congress Cataloging in Publication Data
Lippman, Peter J.   The Know-It-Alls help out.
   Summary: A family of accident-prone alligators try to help a neighbor with her household chores.
   [1. Alligators—Fiction. 2. Helpfulness—Fiction]   I. Title.   PZ7.L666Koh   [E]   81-43431   AACR2
ISBN: 0-385-17397-0   Copyright © 1982 by Peter Lippman
All Rights Reserved   Printed in the United States of America   First Edition

The Know-It-Alls dropped in on their new neighbor one day, and found her washing dishes.

"You must take off your valuable ring before something bad happens to it," said the Know-It-Alls.

"I can't—it's stuck," she replied.

"No problem," said Mother Know-It-All. Ernest squirted some soap on the finger, and Annie and Father pulled.

"Oops!" cried Father Know-It-All as the ring slid off the neighbor's finger, flew through the air and tumbled down the drain. Mother sent Annie and Ernest home to fetch the tools they would need to get it out.

"Don't worry," said the Know-It-Alls as they went to work. "We'll find that ring." Unfortunately the drainpipe snapped just then. "That can be fixed in no time," they said, "but we'll have to rip up a bit of the floor."

They had just torn up enough of the floor to repair the drain when Ernest's crowbar caught between two water pipes. "Hmm," said Father Know-It-All as he reached for a sponge and a mop.

While the neighbor ran down to the cellar to turn off the water, the Know-It-Alls began to break down the kitchen wall. "Follow those pipes," said Ernest. "We'll fix 'em yet."

"Oh, here's the shut-off valve!" shouted the neighbor just as Mother Know-It-All's ax chopped the electrical wires.

"Don't worry about the dark!" the Know-It-Alls yelled back. "We're used to working by candlelight."

"Come on up," they continued, "it'll take only a minute to pull down the ceiling and find out where to attach some new wiring."

However, the hole in the ceiling caused a draft that put out the candle. So, Father Know-It-All started smashing a hole in the outside wall. "This room could use another window," he explained. "We'll put one in later."

The neighbor ran out of her
house because the roof was sagging
dangerously over the hole in the
wall.

"Tut tut," said the Know-It-Alls,
"that's easily taken care of. We'll
just ease the weight off that beam
by removing some of the roof."

After the roof finally caved in, Mother, Father and Ernest were standing around thinking of how they could quickly neaten things up, when Commander Know-It-All drove up in his bulldozer.

The Commander bulldozed everything into a
nice, neat pile. As he went to scoop the last
bucketful of rubble out of the basement, the
Know-It-Alls noticed that Annie was missing.

Just then, she appeared in the bulldozer's scoop, holding up the valuable ring and telling the neighbor not to worry, because the Know-It-Alls were very good at building new houses.